HAVE YOU EVER SEEN A STAR IN THE SEA?

by

CARMELLA NOCCO

Illustrations by

Samantha Paxton

TELEMACHUS PRESS

Cover and interior illustrations by: Samantha Paxton

Published by: Telemachus Press, LLC
www.telemachuspress.com

Visit the author at www.adventuresinstoryland.com

Library of Congress Control Number: 2017931605

ISBN: 978-1-945330-23-0 (eBook)
ISBN: 978-1-945330-24-7 (Paperback)
ISBN: 978-1-945330-25-4 (Hardback)

JUVENILE FICTION

10 9 8 7 6 5 4 3 2 1

2017.05.24

<u>*Dedication*</u>

This story would never have originated without my mother and her love of the beach. This book is dedicated to her, MY SUNSHINE. Through her love, I've learned that memories must be made, they don't just happen. We have shared countless adventures that I will FOREVER hold close to my heart.

Dear Parent/Guardian,

Welcome to <u>Have You Ever Seen A Star in the Sea?</u> My wish is to create a memorable READING ADVENTURE for you and your child. Here's how this adventure is organized…

Once the story begins, you will see a ⭐ or 🦋 🦋 🦋 at the bottom of each page. The 🦋 🦋 🦋 represents places in the story for you to pause in your reading and ask a question. The suggested questions are linked to the "Let's Talk About It!" phrase next to each butterfly. They are leveled and designed to further your child's comprehension and encourage thoughtful responses.

Please share these questions with your child. You will learn a lot about your child as a reader, a learner and a thinker!

I value your input and encourage you to share with others at
www.adventuresinstoryland.com.

Let your READING ADVENTURE begin!
Carmella Nocco

It was a beautiful summer day. Alfred was happy to get back to the beach. He loved playing in the sand and building giant sandcastles. Alfred had all he needed to make *this* castle magnificent.

He had shovels, buckets, shells, dry sand, wet sand and sea water!

Suddenly, Alfred noticed a moving shadow coming closer to him. It reminded him a lot of a penguin.

He looked up and realized it was just his big brother, Daniel.

Daniel wobbled towards him with huge fins on his feet, wearing his big mask and snorkel. Alfred thought Daniel looked silly. But he was happy to see it was Daniel and *NOT A REAL PENGUIN*.

Daniel asked Alfred to go snorkeling with him. He wanted to show him all the different things he saw in the sea. Daniel knew Alfred wasn't interested in fish, shells and seaweed,

so he had to come up with a clever plan to get Alfred to go snorkeling.

Daniel asked, "Hey, do you know what else I saw?" Alfred was curious to hear what his brother was going to say. Daniel blurted, "I saw a STAR in the sea!" Alfred insisted that was impossible. He knew stars were only found in the sky. However, Daniel claimed he saw a star and continued,

"I also saw shiny pearls, mobile homes and vibrant colored trees!"

Instantly, Alfred ran to his mom, shouting, "Can I please have my snorkeling equipment?" "Sure!", said Alfred's mother, as she helped him with his mask and his snorkel. Then he stepped into each fin, one foot at a time.

Alfred and Daniel wobbled down to the water together.

Alfred said, "Hey Dan, *NOWWW* I know why fish choose to swim in the water! These fins sure are difficult to walk in." Daniel looked at Alfred and laughed. As they wobbled to the special snorkeling area, they heard their mother say, "I am watching you, so be careful and remember...safety first!"

Alfred floated in the water
and took his time getting used
to the snorkeling equipment.

Daniel noticed Alfred was more
comfortable and said, "Good job, Al!
Let's begin our adventure!" Alfred
gave him a thumbs up!

As they swam, Alfred was amazed by the
world under the water. He couldn't believe how
quiet and enormous it was. He loved looking
at all the different kinds of fish.

As they swam, Alfred noticed small shiny objects on the bottom of the sea. They swam down to...

As they continued to explore, Alfred was anxious, waiting to see a star in the sea.

He wondered, *will it shine as bright as the stars in the sky?*

Alfred wanted to continue snorkeling. So he asked his little sister, Lucy, to go with him. Lucy didn't want to wear the equipment because it looked too funny. Alfred assured her there was nothing silly about snorkeling, or the equipment.
"After all," he said, "I think it looks super cool!"

Alfred said, "Come on, Lucy. It will be fun!"

Lucy replied, "Nope, sorry."

Let's Talk About It!
Suggested leveled questions

🦋 **Recall details about *Have You Ever Seen a Star in the Sea?***

• Page 24 – What did Alfred see in the water?

• Page 24 – What did Alfred learn about the world under the water?

🦋 **Thoughts about *Have You Ever Seen a Star in the Sea?***

• Page 14 – Why did Daniel laugh at Alfred? Explain.

• Page 23 – Why did Alfred say to Daniel, "I think you're pulling my leg"? Explain.

• Page 28 – How did Alfred persuade Lucy to go snorkeling with him? Explain.

• Page 28 – How did Alfred change in the story? Explain.

🦋 **Bring *Have You Ever Seen a Star in the Sea?* to life and apply it to a child's world**

• Would you like to have gone snorkeling with Daniel? Why?

• How would you persuade someone to go snorkeling with you?

About the Author

Hello, Carmella Nocco here, writing to you from Brooklyn, New York! <u>Have You Ever Seen a Star in the Sea?</u> is my first book. It has a little history of its own, having originated from an elementary education class I took at SUNY New Paltz.

I decided to share this story, because as a school teacher, I witness the magic that happens when children are engaged in good stories. You can see their minds at work and their imaginations soar. I love seeing their smiling faces as laughter fills the room. These moments are the reasons why I've been teaching for 13 years and why I love it.

As a teacher, effective questioning is an essential component of successful lesson planning. Good questions that make connections serve to deepen a child's comprehension of a text. Therefore, I incorporated 3 levels of questioning throughout the story. Great discussions will lead to a memorable *READING ADVENTURE!*

CPSIA information can be obtained at www.ICGtesting.com
Printed in the USA
LVIW01n2318090617
537621LV00005B/25